epic!originals

Undersea Mystery Club

Problem at the Playground

W9-COJ-924

Courtney Carbone

Illustrated by Melanie Demmer

Andrews McMeel
PUBLISHING®

Have you heard about Epic! yet?

We're the largest digital library for kids, used by millions in homes and schools around the world. We love stories so much that we're now creating our own!

With the help of some of the best writers and illustrators in the world, we create the wildest adventures we can think of. Like a mermaid and narwhal who solve mysteries. Or a pet made out of slime.

We hope you have as much fun reading our books as we had making them!

It was a very exciting day in Aquamarina! A new playground was opening, and sea creatures from near and far had come to take part in the fun.

Violet swam up and down, trying to see past the huge crowd of people.

"Can you see what's happening?" she asked her best friend, Wally.

Wally was a narwhal with a long pointy horn like a unicorn. He tried to get a better view but accidentally bumped into a merman in front of him.

"Ouch!" the merman exclaimed, rubbing his tail.

"Oops—sorry!" Wally replied. He sometimes forgot how sharp his horn could be.

Violet offered Wally a supportive smile. So did Dusty, the starfish who lived on top of her hair.

"Let's go this way," Violet said, taking Wally's flipper.

The friends pushed through the crowd, weaving and dodging past merpeople, crustaceans, and fish of all kinds.

Finally, they made their way to the front, where a giant green ribbon blocked off the playground entrance.

The ceremony was about to begin!

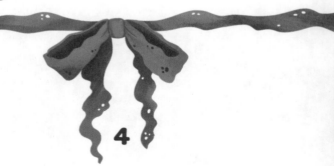

4

2

Violet's mother, the mayor of Aquamarina, stood front and center.

"Welcome one and all to Aquamarina's newest

playground," Mayor Vespera announced. "It's now time for the playground's engineer, Ms. Rivet Rogers, to cut the ribbon and open the park."

Rivet swam forward and pulled a big pair of scissors from her tool kit.

But instead of a *snip*, there was a *clatter*!

The scissors
had fallen apart.

"That's strange," Rivet said, inspecting them. "These scissors are missing a piece."

Violet nudged Wally.

"Maybe we can help!" she offered.

"Yeah!" said Dusty.

Mayor Vespera smiled down at them.

"Wally, will you do the honors?" she asked.

Wally blushed. He didn't like being the center of attention, but

he did like helping out. With a great *swoosh* of his horn, he cut the giant ribbon in half.

Everyone clapped and cheered.

"Aquamarina's new playground is now open!" Mayor Vespera exclaimed.

Suddenly, a terrible rumbling sound came from inside the park.

The clapping and cheering stopped. Everyone looked on in shock as the playground equipment began to fall apart!

Clink! Clang! Clunk!

One by one, the monkey bars fell to the ground.

Ker-plunk!

The swirly slide fell down and rolled to the side.

Crash!

The jungle gym completely collapsed.

Violet rubbed her eyes. She couldn't believe what she was seeing. The park now looked like a giant heap of scrap metal!

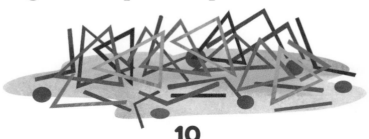

3

"My beautiful park!" Rivet cried. "What happened?"

The mayor quickly stepped in and called everyone to attention.

"It looks like we are having some setbacks," she said. "We will postpone the opening until a later date."

Everyone groaned. A small sea turtle began to sniffle.

Violet thought quickly. She tapped her mom on the shoulder

and whispered something in her ear. The mayor nodded.

"Please come to the Town Hall for refreshments," she announced. "Violet reminded me that our baker has prepared some delicious sea grass cookies."

Everyone forgot all about the park and rushed toward the Town Hall.

"Where do you think you're going?" Violet asked, grabbing hold of Wally's tail as he followed the crowd.

13

"Free cookies!" Wally replied, licking his lips.

"Don't you want to stay and see what happened?"

"Not at much as I want those cookies," Wally admitted.

"Let's see what's going on first,"
Violet said. She waved for him
to follow.

Wally sighed. He knew there
was little chance of cookies in
his future.

A team of security
dolphins arrived on
the scene. They
surrounded the
park with bright
yellow tape.

DANGER DO NOT CROSS

Meanwhile, Mayor Vespera held an emergency meeting with Rivet and her team of engineers.

"I can't believe it!" Rivet exclaimed, picking up a loose monkey bar. "Someone took all the screws, hinges, and nails from my equipment!"

"It must have happened after our final safety check last night," the captain of the security dolphins replied. "Everything was in ship-shape."

"Hmm," said the mayor, inspecting the mess. "It's quite a mystery."

At the word "mystery," Violet's ears perked up. She locked eyes with Wally. They had a lot in common, but the thing they had *most* in common was their love of solving mysteries.

4

"To the clubhouse!" Violet exclaimed.

"To the clubhouse!" Dusty said.

"Yes!" Wally agreed. He had already forgotten all about the sea grass cookies.

The best friends swam to their secret hiding spot, a small alcove in the middle of a nearby coral reef.

"What do you think happened?" Violet asked. She plopped down onto a chair made of sand.

Wally started giggling.

"What's so funny?" she asked.

"The coral is tickling me," Wally said. He wiggled his flippers.

"Wally, we need to focus," Violet said.

"Right," Wally replied. "Do you know what we should do?"

Violet did, indeed.

"A brainstorm!" they exclaimed together.

Coming up with ideas was one of their favorite things to do.

It was also a great way to solve mysteries!

Violet took out an hourglass, a pencil, and her trusty notepad.

"Three, two, one—go!" she said, flipping the hourglass timer over.

Wally had already come up with lots of ideas.

"Maybe an alien submarine came during the night,

and it's part of their plan to take over the world, one park at a time."

Violet laughed and wrote it down.

"Or maybe it was a mad scientist," Wally added, excitedly. "And she used a giant, super-powerful magnet to pull out all the screws and hinges and stuff!"

Violet raised her eyebrow but kept scribbling.

"Or maybe there was an earthquake," Wally suggested.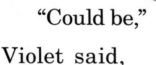

"Could be," Violet said, nodding. "But I think we would have felt that."

"What do you think then?" Wally asked. He was out of ideas.

Violet watched as the last grains of sand passed through the hourglass.

"Well," she said. "Those things are all *possible*. But it's also possible it was just a troublemaker pulling a prank."

"But who would . . . ?" Wally asked, trailing off.

They knew *exactly* who would do such a thing.

"Gill Sharkfin!" they all said at once.

Everyone in Aquamarina knew that Gill Sharkfin was the biggest prankster around. He loved playing tricks on people.

In fact, Gill was so good at pranking he had won the Best Prank award every year since

it had been invented. Of course, he also invented it.

Violet and Wally found Gill right in the middle of town. Not surprisingly, he was moving the hands on the village clock.

"Look who it is!" he said. "Are you here to help me turn back time?"

Violet shook her head.

"We're not here to play games, Gill," she replied. "Someone sabotaged the new playground—"

"And you just assumed it was me?" he cut in.

"It usually *is* you," Violet reminded him.

"True," he replied with a smirk. "And I'm honored. But I can't take credit for this one. My pranks are hilarious, not dangerous. Besides, your mom would exile me if I ruined any more town events this year."

Violet knew he was right. Between Aquamarina's summer parade fiasco, bicentennial blackout, and the silent winter concert, Gill had definitely caused enough trouble already. Not that that would stop him from smaller, everyday pranks.

DING DONG! DING DONG!

The clock chimed so loudly that they all jumped.

A shopkeeper came out of a store across the street.

"Hey!" he called. "Stop messing with that clock."

"Gotta jet!" Gill replied, laughing. "See ya around!"

He swam off in a flash of bubbles.

Violet and Wally slowly swam back to their clubhouse.

"Now what?" Wally asked. "That was our only good lead."

Violet thought about the clock striking twice.

"That's it!" she exclaimed. "If the culprit struck once, they may strike again!"

Wally clapped his flippers.

"Meet me at the playground tonight after dinner," Violet explained. "We have to go back to the scene of the crime. If Gill— or someone else—comes back, we'll be ready for them."

6

Later that night, Violet and Wally returned to the park.

"We need a hideout to catch the thief in the act," Violet told him.

Wally used his horn to reveal a mermaid- and narwhal-size hole in a wall of seaweed.

"How about here?" he asked. "It's my favorite hide-and-seek spot."

"Perfect!" Violet replied. "And good to know," she added with a wink.

"Oops!" Wally sighed.

Soon the friends were hidden from view. The long wait had begun.

"I'm hungry," Wally complained.

"You're always hungry," Violet laughed. "But I have something for you."

She reached into her backpack and pulled out a brown bag.

"Do you know what you eat during a stakeout?" she asked.

"Steak!" Wally cried.

"Um, no," Violet laughed. "But I did bring you some leftover sea grass cookies."

Wally smiled as he gobbled up the cookies.

The sun was slowly disappearing overhead.

"Ugh!" Wally grunted. "This is taking forever. Shouldn't the aliens be here by now?"

Violet laughed.

"We have to be patient," she said. "Besides, it's only been a little while."

"I hope they come soon," Wally said. "I have to be home by dark."

"Me too," she sighed.

"Me three!" added Dusty.

Crunch. Crunch. Crunch.

"What's that noise?"
Violet whispered,
putting a hand
to her ear.
"Is someone
out there?"

Wally stopped
chewing.

"No," he replied, his mouth
full. "I just finished the bag
of cookies."

"I think it was something else,"
Violet replied. "Quick! Toss me
those binoculars!"

41

Wally used his horn to flip the binoculars to Violet.

The last glimmers of sunlight beamed off the metal heap in the middle of the park. Violet adjusted her binoculars just in time to see something move in the moonlight.

"What are those things?" Violet whispered.

"Aliens!" Wally replied. "I knew it all along."

"They look like rocks," Violet said.

"Alien rocks!" Wally added.

Violet slapped her hand to her forehead.

"We have to get a closer look," she said. "I'm going in."

Wally gulped. He knew that meant he was going in, too.

Violet swam quietly toward
the objects, with Wally right
behind. They watched in shock as
the mysterious rocks began
to remove hinges, screws,
and other shiny objects
from the playground!

Violet handed half of the net to Wally.

"Three . . . two . . . one," she counted down. "Now!"

In a flash, she and Wally dropped the net on the thieves.

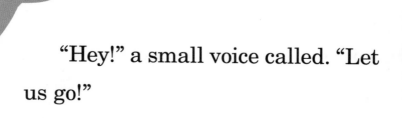

"Hey!" a small voice called. "Let us go!"

Violet swam down lower to see the tiny objects up close.

"You can talk?" she asked.

"Of course, we can talk," one rock replied. "We're decorator crabs."

Violet and Wally looked at each other in surprise. The rocks weren't rocks at all!

8

"**W**hat are you doing here?" Violet asked. "Why are you taking parts from the playground?"

"What do you mean?" the crab replied. "We've been collecting things from this place for years. No one ever cared before."

"That's because it wasn't a playground before," Violet said.

"Well, nobody told us," said another crab, in a very crabby tone. "We couldn't tell what it was from all the way down here, you know."

"Didn't you see all the sea creatures here today?" Wally asked.

The crabs laughed.

"Of course not," a different crab replied. "We're nocturnal. We only come out at night."

Violet nodded. Finally, it all made sense.

"We collect things to cover and camouflage our bodies," the leader added.

"Camouflage means hide!" added a young crab. "That's how we stay safe."

"Well, for everyone to stay safe," Violet said, "we need you to stop taking parts of the playground equipment. Everything is falling apart because of the missing pieces."

"Okay, okay," said the first crab, reluctantly. "We didn't realize we were causing trouble. We'll stop. Just please let us loose!"

Rivet and the other engineers arrived early the next morning to repair the playground. To their surprise, Violet, Wally, Dusty, and the crabs were already there with all of the missing pieces!

"We're sorry for ruining your playground," the leader of the crabs told Rivet. "We won't take things from here anymore, and we can help rebuild the playground."

"Thank you for your apology," Rivet replied. "We could use your help!"

She handed the crabs some tiny
screwdrivers and wrenches.

"Now let's get started. We have
a new park to build!"

Everyone got to work rebuilding
the playground.

Word about what had happened quickly spread around town.

Violet's friends and neighbors from all over Aquamarina came to help out. Even Gill pitched in! (Sort of.)

In the end, the playground passed a thorough new safety inspection.

There were even enough leftover parts for the decorator crabs to take some home.

The park was ready for a grand reopening!

The big day had arrived—again. Everyone gathered to enjoy the new playground.

Mayor Vespera greeted the crowd.

"Citizens of Aquamarina," she began. "Without further ado,

I'm delighted to welcome you to our new town park!"

The crowd clapped and cheered even louder than before.

Rivet stepped forward with the big pair of scissors, which had been fixed when the crabs returned the missing bolt.

"Designing and building this park has made me very proud," Rivet said. "But seeing how the town came together to set things right truly makes this playground even more special than I ever imagined."

Violet reached out and took Wally's flipper. She was proud, too.

"That said," the engineer went on, "none of this would have been possible without the help of two brave super-sleuths who solved the playground mystery."

Rivet patted Violet and Wally on the shoulder.

"Violet and Wally, thank you for all of your hard work, bravery, and quick thinking," Rivet continued. The crowd exploded into applause.

The two friends looked at each other in surprise. Neither one had expected this!

Swoosh!

Rivet, Violet, and Wally cut the green ribbon together.

With a cheer, the crowd streamed into the playground.

They were laughing and having fun on all of the shiny new equipment in no time.

"What a perfect park," said Violet.

"Excellent work, everyone," agreed Mayor Vespera. "But I noticed there's one thing missing."

Rivet's face dropped.

"I triple-checked everything!" she said. "What could possibly be wrong?"

"You forgot to build a sandbox," Mayor Vespera replied. Then she burst out laughing.

Everyone laughed with her, because they all knew that Aquamarina was already completely covered in sand.

Undersea Mystery Club

More to Explore

Decorator Crabs

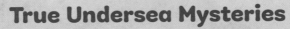

Decorator crabs are organisms who live in the ocean and collect things to decorate or camouflage themselves. They can be up to 5 inches wide and are found all over the world. There is not one specific species of decorator

crab, but instead many different types that have the same behavior.

Like in this story, decorator crabs find items to attach to their bodies: seaweed, shells, gravel, algae, and sponges (the sea kind). Curved, bristlelike hairs called setae catch onto the items to make them stick. This helps the crabs blend in with their environment and keep them safe.

Civil Engineers

An engineer is someone who designs, invents, and constructs things, like machines and buildings, to make our lives safer and easier.

They invent robots, work on new medicines, create computer software, and even build spaceships!

Civil engineers, like Rivet, are able to create large structures like parks and playgrounds. Maybe one day you can become an engineer and build something that helps people, too!

Narwhals

Narwhals like Wally are a type of whale with a long spiral "tusk." This ivory hornlike feature is actually a protruding tooth, which comes from the left side of the jaw, and grows right through the lip! The tusks are most common in males, though females sometimes grow them as well. Occasionally, narwhals can grow two tusks!

These mysterious creatures can range from 13 to 20 feet long (not including the tusk), which is similar in size to cars and trucks you see on the highway. A single narwhal can weigh thousands of pounds and live to be over 50 years old! They live in Arctic waters and eat ocean organisms like fish and squid.

About the Author

Courtney Carbone studied English and Creative Writing in the United States and Australia before becoming a children's book writer and editor in New York City. Her favorite things include trivia nights, board games, stand-up comedy, bookstores, brick-oven pizza, and sharks.

About the Illustrator

Melanie Demmer attended the College for Creative Studies in Detroit, where she earned a BFA in illustration. Currently based in Los Angeles, she creates artwork digitally but also enjoys using watercolor, markers, colored pencils, and acrylic paint. Melanie loves to create bright, colorful illustrations with a variety of textures.

Problem at the Playground

Andrews McMeel Publishing
a division of Andrews McMeel Universal
1130 Walnut Street, Kansas City, Missouri 64106

www.andrewsmcmeel.com

Epic! Creations, Inc.
702 Marshall Street, Suite 280, Redwood, California 94063

www.getepic.com

19 20 21 22 23 BGP 10 9 8 7 6 5 4 3 2 1

Paperback ISBN: 978-1-5248-5524-6
Hardback ISBN: 978-1-5248-5547-5

Library of Congress Control Number: 2019942381

Design by Wendy Gable, Andrea Modica, and Dan Nordskog

Made by:
Bang Printing
Address and location of manufacturer:
3323 Oak Street
Brainard, Minnesota 56401
1st Printing—8/2/19

ATTENTION: SCHOOLS AND BUSINESSES
Andrews McMeel books are available at quantity discounts with bulk purchase for educational, business, or sales promotional use. For information, please e-mail the Andrews McMeel Publishing Special Sales Department: specialsales@amuniversal.com.

Look for more adventures with the

Undersea Mystery Club

COMING SOON!